Christmas Presence
a Call

By Michael Wanchena

Barb -
Thanks for your
presence among us.
Michael

Copyright © 2001 by Michael Wanchena
Published by Christmas Presence Partners, P.O. Box 1039, Delano, Minnesota 55328-1039 USA

All rights reserved. No part of this book may be reproduced or transmitted in any form or by any means, electronic or mechanical, including photocopying, recording, or by any information storage and retrieval system, without permission in writing from the publisher.

ISBN: 0-9713997-0-0

Book design by Peggy Lauritsen Design Group, Minneapolis, Minnesota
Photography by Steve Wewerka, St. Paul, Minnesota, 651-917-7929
Cover photo by Don Farrall for PhotoDisc®
Quote on page 8 from *Native American Wisdom*, Kent Nerburn, editor, New World Library, 1991, p. 42.

Preface

Gracie Allen said that she was so surprised when she was born…that she didn't speak for a year and a half. I understand.

The only possible excuse for this little book is that I am vain enough to think that it may make someone's life a bit easier. I have been spared, wonderfully, the life of either a trained theologian or philosopher. This is 'inspirational' literature, which means, I think, that one need have no particular qualifications in order to publish. I have a modest liberal arts education, I pray, I listen, and I watch and talk.

I approach you from many times and places, from the coral reefs of the Florida Keys and the majesty of the northern Rockies, from the hallowed ground of Assisi and the cacophony of Chinatown in New York City, from the sweltering heat of Hong Kong and the frozen tundra of the North. I joined the Marine Corps in 1968, then joined thousands of veterans as we protested in Washington, D.C. during the spring of 1970. I have labored in asylums that housed unholy pain, disfigurement and misery, sailed merchant sea vessels exploring for oil, loaded baggage on Greyhound buses and sold millions of dollars of investment securities. I am an inventor and entrepreneur, an unpublished novelist and a pretty decent weeder of gardens. I have been physically beaten within moments of life's end, have raised two very special sons, and lived with the same, singularly remarkable woman for nearly thirty years. Disease, death and addiction have left their handprints upon me, as have love, mercy and laughter. I pray that I arrive at Heaven's Gate sweating and bleeding, snot-smeared and torn, dirtied and exhausted, breathless and, finally, happily, without words.

Well away from my home in Minnesota, a stone's throw from the Gulf of Mexico, I inelegantly sat, poised upon an increasingly wobbly barstool, nearly a year ago now, flanked by my wife, Patricia, and an old friend, Bill, a saintly scoundrel who lives among the poor in Tampa. Trying to summarize my life, the three of us sipped Long Island Iced Teas until, well, until we couldn't. I turned fifty years old that night, and made the decision that I'd write this little book one day. This summary of one man's lifetime of learnings has come sooner than expected, and of course I underestimated the time involved.
This has taken way more than a day.

The inspiration for Christmas Presence is a clear, decade old , quiet prompting in my spirit, its confirmation, the uncountable number of souls who have touched my life.
My mother Shirley, is an indomitable force of love and hope.
Father Urban Wagner has been my friend and spiritual director for more than ten years, he has become my benchmark of saintly, modern manhood.

I owe special thanks to my editor, Steve Polansky, who crawled inside my heart and head, roamed around and with practiced skill and grace, teased and coaxed the best he could from me.
The failings in this little book are, mea culpa, *mine alone.*

Most of all, I owe my intimate and devoted thanks to Patricia, Jason and Dominic.
They alone can know why.

to
Veronica Christine Wanchena,
And to You

We do not want churches because they will teach us to quarrel about God, as the Catholics and Protestants do. We do not want to learn that. We may quarrel with men sometimes about things on this earth. But we never quarrel about God. We do not want to learn that.

—CHIEF JOSEPH, NEZ PERCE

Christmas Presence is God with skin on.

Through simple acts of courtesy, respect, humility and mercy we become, moment to moment, the hands and feet, the listening heart or broken silence of God. By our billions we can choose to live as the eternal beings we are: eternal souls who journey, enfleshed and time bound, within a human experience. By our humble, common, virtuous actions and restraints, Christmas Presence can transform our world. In genuine communal-union the faithful, practiced living of Christmas Presence can transform history through its quiet war against exhaustion, apathy, fear, and predatory evil.

The scandal of Christianity is that we say we believe, individually and as a community, that God is present in our hands and feet, in our listening and speaking, but then we behave as if this were not at all true. What can God do with my hands and feet as I watch television in the dark? With my mind and heart? What can God do with the cashier at the coffee shop if I do not meet his eyes, do not say a silent prayer of thanksgiving for his presence and protection for his journey? What if the Spirit led me into an encounter with another eternal being, an immortal soul fashioned outside of time yet breathed into time, and I witnessed this soul hauling trash, or drunk in a corner, or hiring me for a job? What if this immortal soul were a Chairman of the Board, or dangerously cutting me off in traffic? Or a man with a gun? How would I behave?

The central moment of the Christmas Presence experience is one of profoundly intimate, personal freedom: the freedom to behave either according to our lasting or our temporary natures. Because we are all human, how we respond to this freedom is often, and necessarily, a muddled mix of animal instinct and angelic whispers. This is what I mean, and how I broke my Christmas Presence heart one afternoon last summer.

Backing into Christmas Presence

In another lifetime my friend Steve J. would have been the town blacksmith. These days he re-shoes cars. His hands seem the size of baseball gloves, grease stained and heavily calloused. Thirty years ago those same hands were young, iron hard and whisper quick; they won Golden Glove fights. Steve laughs easily, his banter is uncomplicated, his generous stories about the local folk and life often funny. He and I coached our sons for a few summers of baseball. Steve's knowledge of the game is remarkable, the pleasure he takes from it, infectious.

His tire shop is small-town quaint, a cluttered and happily busy place as townsfolk come and go, Steve replacing and fixing tires, changing oil, bantering with the relaxed confidence and ease of a man who knows his work and takes pleasure in it. Steve is one of the good guys. I enjoy hanging out there, particularly after a messy session smithing words. Jerking my head from the clouds and getting my hands a bit dirty is, for me, a cultivated survival skill. Into this easy setting, on a hot August afternoon, wanders a door-to-door salesman. "Now who's this," asks Steve of me, eyes aglitter, an easy smile forming on his leathery face.

Hurt not others in ways that you yourself would find hurtful.

— UDANA-VARGA 5.1

Ours is a small town of twenty-five hundred people. Steve knows everyone. The salesman's short-sleeved shirt is buttoned to the top, his tie, handsomely knotted. He doesn't appear bothered by the heat, which is oppressive, and he's quick with a smile. And I immediately begin to screw up the whole encounter.

"Hey." I withhold a handshake, feigning dirt and grease. "Wachha got?" For some reason I feel like teasing this guy. He's such an easy, milquetoast mark, and I'm feeling playful.

"I'm selling rubber stamps," he says, opening an inexpensive sample case he's rested on the top of an alignment machine. I reply that I've got all the rubber stamps I'll ever need, look him in the eye, and in the way of men, I size him up.

There are all kinds of gentle ways to be a jerk. The details of this encounter, like the pain of labor and delivery, are mercifully obscured. In a bewildering couple of minutes I do know that I gave this man a little grief and pushed him away. No passerby would have noticed, but Steve blinked. With my spirit and body language I pushed the rubber stamp selling man, with careless words and expressions I cut him.

He was leaving now, wounded because a small-town guy demeaned and bullied him. His expression conveyed a thousand words. I had a sick feeling as this man, a perfectly fine man honestly working at an innocent job, turned to leave and looked me hard in the eye. "Why?" was his unasked question. His hurt and confusion, his accusation, were knife edge keen. "Why did you do this?"

I honestly do not know why. And as I drove home the thought occurred to me that perhaps I, Mr. Christmas Presence, had just turned away, cruelly, an angel selling rubber stamps.

Instead of turning into my driveway I backed away and drove the streets anxiously looking for this rubber stamp selling man, cussing myself for my sin. I thought about this man's wife and kids, about his little league team, about his hopes and dreams. After twenty minutes of crisscrossing town, I gave up. I wanted to say I was sorry, to ask his forgiveness. I wanted to buy a rubber stamp. I wouldn't be given that satisfaction. I prayed that afternoon for forgiveness. I found myself smack in the middle of Christmas Presence, a haunting moment I'll cherish the rest of my life. I feel forgiven as now, instead, I journey with my rubber stamp selling companion forever.

We live, nailed upon the earth. Souls trapped in hungry and decaying bodies; our machines outlive us. We sense that both Caesar and God are due their due, and offer each a confusion of silence, tears, laughter, of sweat, prayer, and Budweiser. It is true and obvious that we have been born into the raw, mortal pond of the Neverlasting. It is true, but not so immediately obvious, that we also dwell in the invisible stream of the Everlasting. It is, then, no paradox that both Homer Simpson and his hysterical world, and Teresa, that holy woman of Calcutta, are cultural icons.

In purely Christian terms Christmas Presence is the experience of the Incarnation of God in the world: The Holy Spirit, God, has left the temple and taken up residence in his people (see Paul and his Damascan ride into history). Christmas Presence is an awareness of the living, spiritual bloodline that binds all of us, in our billions, moment to moment, to the Heart of Love.

The beginning and end of the Torah is performing acts of loving kindness.

—TALMUD: SOTAH, 14A

The experience of Christmas Presence is not limited to the Christian community. The Bethlehem Star shone not only over the dusty little manger, its light permeated time and space. The language of Christmas Presence is beautifully, and unavoidably, Christian, yet it is absolutely universal in its desire and experience. At its finest, Christmas Presence becomes the passageway through which miracles of the heart, the hands, and the spirit can flow.

Christmas Presence is the 'ah-ha' of my soul, and the actions of my soul, consequent to the realization that God has chosen humankind as his doorway into the perceptible universe. We are, literally in our billions, the residence of God's hands and feet, his eyes and ears, his heart and spirit. Christmas Presence is an awareness that our private, and not so private, acts cause ripples that move out into the seen and unseen world, thereby sustaining an ancient, quiet war against suffering and evil.

"WWJD" is an acronym that crept into our culture with no organized effort. The question "What would Jesus do?" was appreciated by Christians of all ilk. "WWJD" has become a modern icon that projects me, in seeing it, into the heart of the matter: it is exactly the right question. Our answer to that question, if not boisterous, is non-negotiable: "Christmas Presence is what Jesus would do."

God in the Dust

I close my eyes, still myself, and conjure an image of nighttime in the desert. The moon is a sliver high in the sky, the stars are spilled from sky's edge to sky's edge, ablaze in the dark cold. I am lying on my side, atop a roughly woven cape, my head fills with the smoky aromas of a dying fire. Around me, littering the landscape, are other shadowed sleepers. Just in front of me, on his side with his back to me, is Jesus. I watch the rhythmic movement of his breathing, am startled by an occasional twitch or spasm. He snores lightly, and sometimes speaks words I cannot understand. I think back to earlier in the day. Who is this man? I pick a gospel story, and insert myself in the middle of it. Usually I am an observer. I stare, variously engaged, perplexed, astounded, and giggling. Sometimes I am the woman who frantically finds and touches the hem of his robe, or a confounded religious leader. I might be his mother, both frightened and in awe. Or a rotting leper. Too infrequently are mine the hands that heal, the eyes that call to life and light.

I rode into Jesus' life in a Studebaker, it and I each scrubbed shiny for Sunday Mass. Swathed in the incense and candles, the Gregorian chant and the vestments and rhythms of penitential Roman Catholicism, my first and most indelible image of God is as a Broken Jesus. God in the dust. God, run to ground. I recall, as an altar boy, standing stock still, transfixed, as waves of incense rose around me, as our priest prayed the Stations of the Cross, the final journey of Jesus through the streets of Jerusalem.

I've fallen, if not always gracefully, in love with my bleeding, salty God in the dust. Fumbling toward ecstasy. From the little league fields on the north side of town, to the office where I work, from the newspapers and television to my quiet prayer time: "There," I point (lovingly, excitedly, reprovingly, and confounded), "is Jesus."

*Faith is always at a disadvantage;
it is a perpetually defeated thing which
survives all its conquerors.*

—GK CHESTERTON

I grew up with the wonder-filled iconography of my faith: the Sacred Heart of Jesus, the Stations of the Cross, the Dashboard Jesus, Jesus on the walls and in the books, Jesus hanging from my neck, from every doorway threshold. And though the iconography has disappeared from my thresholds, the images of Jesus remain, they are the filter through which I see and understand myself and the world. I've got a case of Jesus on the brain. Jesus as an idea, as a concept. I can chat happily and convincingly about Jesus and black holes, about Jesus and innocent suffering, about Jesus and you, about Jesus and anything.

It is poetic fact that the longest eighteen inches in the world is the distance from one's heart to one's brain. A sad consequence of Jesus on the brain is that I keep praying for him to fix the world around me, and not to fix me. A survey of the evening news leaves me feeling that Christianity is like a professional football team that hasn't won a championship for two thousand years. I'm weary to the bone of looking and feeling like a loser, me and my invisible quarterback.

Christ victorious? We have poisoned the air and waters of our planet; unending, complicated noises and violent images pour into our homes; worldwide millions upon millions of human beings are literally ignored to death. Genocide, fratricide, suicide. Racism, sexism, nationalism and churchism cut and divide us, divvy the pitiable spoil amongst the strong. Then do it again. Teresa, that holy woman of Calcutta, said that it is a great poverty that children must die so that we might live as we do.

These violent, evil realities exist in large part because Jesus is solely an idea for many Christians, and not a physical, living reality, as for instance the 'realness' of the next person you encounter, say, a door-to-door rubber stamp salesman. This is not to demean the power or importance of ideas, and as ideas go, Jesus is an idea of unparalleled power and excellence. But having or nurturing a good idea ('George Washington') is not the same as living with George Washington, of having George Washington as a soul mate. Of doing George's laundry.

I exist two thousand years from the Palestinian man-in-time Jesus, who was, we plead, God enfleshed. All this time, and all these books and stories and pictures, all these saints and sinners, exist, layered in an enormous space between me and him. Yet, if I am to believe Jesus, and those women and men who knew the man most intimately, he is just as real and alive, even more so, today, than he could have been in ancient Nazareth. Whereas the Galilean carpenter, Jesus, was confined by space and time as you and I are, today and forevermore he is universally available as The Christ.

The mystery and the implications of the Incarnation have driven me, at times, to my limits with joy and suffering, clarity and chaos. If God is God and he can do anything, I suppose I must concede the possibility of Incarnation. But even if God can do this thing, why would he?

Words that come from the heart enter the heart.

—MOSES IBN EZRA, SHIRAT YISRAEL

God With Skin On

Ronald Rolheiser tells a wonderful story told about a four-year-old girl who, alone in her room one night, becomes frightened of monsters and goblins and such. She soon scurries down the hall to her parents' room, and mother kindly and gently takes the little girl back down the hall, reassuring her that there are no spooks or monsters. Anyway, explains mother as she tucks her daughter back in bed, checking the closet for her, "you never need to worry because God is always right here in the room with you." Her daughter quickly retorts, "I know God is in the room with me…but I need someone with some skin on."

We each need God with skin on. The scandal of the Incarnation of God is not just a singular historical fact, vested in the time of Jesus. It is an almost unthinkable, ongoing reality. We are the Body. We are, each one of us, eternal spirits, exquisitely bound in flesh, who, for a brief flowering of time, have been chosen to house the holy.

Like Elvis, God has fled the building: no longer is God to be found exclusively in the Ark, in the Temple, on the Mountaintop. Rather, we are the temples of God's residence. He has chosen us as his doorways into his creation. To perform his miracles, to feed the hungry and clothe the naked, to comfort the lonely and imprisoned, to move mountains of hopelessness and despair, of violence and apathy, he reaches out with our hands, our hearts and minds.

This is what drove the enraged Saul of Tarsus blind: the staggering realization that it was Christ himself whom he persecuted. It took the renegade rabbi, Saul-Paul, years to begin to write what it meant: that the enfleshment of God had not only taken place in the historical person of Jesus, it continues, it is extended by each one of God's human creations, this mysterious being we call the Mystical Body of Christ.

We are surely made in the image and likeness of God. But in what respect? Certainly it is in this respect: our 'be-ing', that non-physical force we call spirit/soul which animates our physical body, is the likeness of God. My image of God, the God of my mind's eye, is predictably fatherly; my experience of God, God with skin on, God encountered in the woof and weave of my life, is distinctly maternal. I blame Shirley for that.

When I think of my mother there is little of her physical image, which has changed much in fifty years, that comes to mind. When I think of Shirley, I think not in words, but in watercolors. My mother is the poetry of love, the amazement of a child, the burly, gentle cop who cares. Her love for me, however harshly tested, never wavers an inch. It is her spirit, her personality, the depth and wisdom of her unflinching love, the test of her character over time that fills my senses. It is this animated force, this glowing, pulsing soul, 'mother', whom I know and love, who has known and loved me.

It is this animated force we name 'soul' that God has fashioned in his likeness. The invisible urge to connect, to love, to be loved is the likeness of God. The sight of a mother nursing a child, or a family noisily engaged in a meal, a colleague intensely engaged in work, or any of a thousand other scenes reveal to us the image of God. Loving, sharing, mixing it up and working it out: this is how we see God daily.

God is love.
Love is a verb.

*No one of you is a believer until
he desires for his brother that which he
desires for himself.*

—SUNNAH

Christmas Presence

I want to trade my Christmas presents in for Christmas Presence. I want to participate in a New Christmas. A Christmas without calendar and religious borders, a Christmas celebration that erupts daily, as unexpectedly and humbly as that first day of God in the Flesh. A Christmas celebration that understands that peace and joy and brotherhood can be experienced, but only after the fact—the fact that we are loved, loved to death, and that each of us must love each of us to death.

For ten years I have been signing the infrequent Christmas cards I send, '…and thank you for your Christmas Presence in my life.' It was the month before Christmas, and I was staying in guest quarters at St. John's Abbey in Collegeville, Minnesota. About four o'clock one morning, smoking in a huddled fit outside the Abbey door, I was trying to decide to whom I should make out Christmas cards. There are about two hundred to-whom's I'd like to mail each year, but I usually manage actually to post only five or so: my intentions are characteristically bigger than my attentions. I had a thought and hurried back to the table where I jotted it down. Christmas Presence. A turn of words, crafted to gently rebuke what has become, in America, a season of consumer madness. Intended to, at least for this moment, pierce through the din of Madison Avenue advertisers, and in doing so, by reminding you of your sacredness, perhaps make a smidgen of difference.

An unexpected consequence of this exercise in wordplay has been a slow, excruciatingly personal gravitation into the mystery of the Incarnation. I catch myself in little daily events, muttering a whispered 'Christmas Presence' as I witness or participate in such a thing: this recognition of the resident divine and its transmission from one to another in small, generally hidden or silent acts of mercy.

This transmission of sanctity, of grace, through our acts, is as simple as this:

A young boy gives his mother a big hug one morning, and this pleases his mother so much that she makes her husband his favorite breakfast. The husband is so delighted with his breakfast that he tips the parking lot attendant that morning. The attendant, not used to tips of any kind, is happy to buy lunch for a friend, who later goes home and helps his wife with the dishes. She's so pleased at their little conversation over the dishes that later that evening, after the kids are in bed, she suggests a little lovin'. Nine months later new life enters the world.

The power of this little story, of this meditation, brings us into the heart of Christmas Presence:

This profound state of awareness that Christian Spirituality, if not incarnate, if not rooted in my neighbor, is an uprooted, fallen, tree. Like the little boy who gave his mommy love one morning, I must hug, I must move onward, trusting the echoes of my passing presence.

God, still salty, sweating, bleeding and in the dust, dwells this and every moment in the swollen sea of hungering humanity. He is wherever they are. Christmas Presence is a meditation which will lead you to Him, in Them, prompting your hands and feet, eyes and ears, into small, random, acts of kindness and faith, acts of silence and laughter, of listening and leaping, each day. As our acts echo into creation, the idea of Jesus among us becomes the hands and feet, the fleshy miracle of Jesus among us.

Christmas Presence.

Pass it on.

Afterword

Early July, 2001

In middle May of 2001, as this little essay went into pre-publication design and layout, and in anticipation of the tremendous amount of effort and love the launching my new business would require, I felt suddenly and absolutely compelled to make a 30-day 'desert' retreat. Jesus' first reaction to the announcement of his ministry was to hightail it to the desert. Certainly there was a lesson there for me. It was not an anxiety-filled search for big or little answers, but an opportunity, perhaps singular in my lifetime, to maintain a new level of silence and solitude, of frequent and unfettered prayer time, of rest and reflection, of 'peeling away the layers, seeing what was left.'

I had not planned for this event. It caught me decidedly off guard and left me feeling vulnerable. It seemed, in an odd and fascinating way, 'Old Testament', this call to me for a passive, bloody sacrifice of myself before Him. I would be led mute, shorn of the protections offered by my computer, Diet Coke and cigarettes, stripped of telephone, television, family and friends, into a remarkably ancient and sacred desert place where there is only life and death.

The doors flew open, nearly torn from their hinges, to this prompting, and within days of making the decision, I left home in Delano, Minnesota and drove my shiny red Durango, muttering and wondering along the thirteen-hundred-mile drive, to Christ in the Desert Monastery, a Benedictine monastic community located deep within the Chama Wilderness area of the New Mexico high desert. Located thirty miles from Abique, the monastery can be found at the end of Forest Service Road #151, a barely marked, rutted and serpentine dirt road that will challenge even four-wheel-drive vehicles, and which often becomes impassable during the afternoon rains of July and August.

'Christ in the Desert' is wonderfully named. It is a place where the desert and the mountains meet, where the silent and unforgiving canyon walls bleed red sandstone, where the quiet rhythm of prayer, work and study grind at one's soul like the wet, gritty silicone in a lapidarian tumbler of pretty stones. There, at 6500 feet above sea level, in the geologic majesty of that which will never know them, in the presence of the God who indwells, the monks and nuns of Christ in the Desert are slowly sloshing away, tumbling hour by hour, day upon week upon year, into shiny souls.

I am writing another book about my time there, but there is a story, or at least a punch line, which I must share with you today.

We each have our own story. I've got mine, you've got yours. We can tell it in fifteen or twenty minutes, tweaking it a bit for an employer, marriage counselor, priest or bartender, for our families and friends. Mostly we tell our story to ourselves. And this is a good thing. We must reflect on our lives, give them shape and meaning. At times we must be able to convey this story, in words, to other people. But it is just my story. The story I tell to myself about myself will not, for example, be the story others tell about me.

There is a psychological test that is done with black and white silhouettes: an example is a picture of two faces, shadow cutouts in profile, mirroring each other. If you gaze at the picture long enough, or know the trick, you can see that the white space between the images is in the shape of a chalice, or vase. In the seeing of the white space the black silhouetted faces don't disappear, and they vanish. It is a wonderful, childlike apprehension to discover the white space, the chalice.

By the tenth day of my retreat I had come to a halt. It was a bit like docking the Queen Mary, but I did manage to shut up and slow down enough that as I looked about, even the monks seemed in a hurry. Sadness lapped at my edges. I wasn't exactly sad, but I could see it coming. I was tired. I was eating, by choice, one, usually small, meal a day. Not smoking. Not writing. I had walked the canyon for hours each day, muttering the Jesus prayer, or letting my mind drift. I contemplated the same two small passages of scripture day after day. My sleep, usually world-class, had become fractured and desperate. By the end of the second week I was moving in a deep, fog-like sadness. I wanted to leave. There is wonderful detail and drama in this time, but that is not for now. Let me say simply that on that dusty road, an hour's walk from the monestary, *in a flash*, *in quick gasp of air*, I apprehend the white space of my life.

My story, the one I tell you and me, is the two faces in silhouette. God's story is the white space in between. The Chalice. It's exactly the same and exactly different.

I have led a colorful life. Not all the colors have been lovely or true. Like yours, my story is by turns tragic and comic, gripping and dull. A salesman and entrepreneur my entire life, I have left family and cave, hunting mammoth but bringing back rabbit. My scars are deep, I am often freshly wounded. But I laugh a lot, and I don't seem to run out of hope. I have told a dark, mysterious and wonderful, but ultimately sad story of the hunt. And happily it is sadness to which my God has drawn me in the desert. Gray, formless, mind-numbing sadness.

Then this: one second I'm locked in tears and exhaustion, the next I see my life in panorama, from git to go. And I see it from God's eyes. Like yours, it is a life of heroism, of love and faithfulness and courage. It is a drama of might and majesty. And this is the thing: I see this, shudder with mountain-top delight and how do I respond? I pretty much plop my tired butt down on Forest Road #151 and laugh. Bubbling delight and joy that is pure as gold. It is good that I was speechless. There was nothing left to say.

I have spoken to you about Christmas Presence. About the little lights and the little acts. This is just a note to you, loved one, that our lights add up, they grow and become the contours of white space, God's story, within the shadows.

The Psalmist has sung, "They are like trees planted near streams of water: they yield fruit in due season, their leaves will never whither." Believe.

Pass it on,

Michael Wanchena
At my home in Delano, Minnesota

Michael Wanchena is a Marine Corps veteran and graduate of the University of Minnesota. A writer, public speaker, inventor and private businessperson, Mr. Wanchena is the founder and chairman of Wedgewood Golf, Inc., a Minneapolis, Minnesota-based golf equipment company. A volunteer at Pacem in Terris, a Franciscan hermitage retreat center located in Isanti, Minnesota, he resides in Delano, Minnesota with his wife, Patricia. He has two sons, Jason and Dominic.

For additional copies of this book,
Or additional information,
Please visit us on the World Wide Web:
mychristmaspresence.com

Or contact us at:

Christmas Presence Partners
Post Office Box 1039
Delano, Minnesota 55328-1039
USA
Telephone: 763-972-3001